For Ewan, John Graham, and Cameron

First Troll printing 2002.

Copyright © 1995 by Elizabeth Rodger.

Published by Troll Communications L.L.C.

ISBN 0-8167-7592-3

Printed in the United States of America.

10 9 8 7 6 5 4 3 2 1

Christmas without a Tree

Elizabeth Rodger

Troll

Christmas was coming.
Snow had been falling softly and quietly during the night.
The Pig family set off to find a tree at the tree farm.
The Pig children, Sally, Toby, and Charlie, were having fun in the fresh snow.

At the farm, the Pigs found short trees
and tall trees, thin trees and thick trees.
None was quite right.

Then Charlie, the youngest pig, found a
perfect little pine tree—fat, bushy, and round.
Father chopped it down with his ax.

Charlie put his nose to
the tree and sniffed the
wonderful pine smell. It
was the smell of Christmas.

On their way home, the Pig family came upon Grumpy Gramps Badger shoveling a path through the snow.

"Hello, Mr. Badger. Look at our perfect tree," called Charlie, proud of his find.

"Humph! What's so perfect about a tree?" grumbled Grumpy Gramps, scarcely lifting his head.

Without another word, Grumpy Gramps shuffled slowly up the path into his dark, quiet house. No wreath hung on his door. No Christmas tree sparkled in his window.

Christmas wasn't coming to the house of Grumpy Gramps.

How very sad, thought Charlie.

At home, Father Pig cut branches from the bottom of the little pine tree. Now it would fit easily into the tree stand.

Mother Pig used some of the branches to make a wreath.
As Charlie watched Mother, he thought of Grumpy Gramps.
Christmas wouldn't come to Grumpy Gramps if he didn't have
a wreath.

Mother Pig helped Charlie make a wreath.
He decorated it with crab apples, holly berries,
pine cones, and a big red bow.
It was very pretty.

Charlie put on his coat
and hat. Mother tied his scarf
snugly around his neck.
Then he set off to take the
wreath to Grumpy Gramps.

Charlie was scared when he reached the house of Grumpy Gramps. No light shone in the window. All was dark and quiet. Slowly, quietly, he crept along the path on tiptoes.

He was sure the door would fly open and Grumpy Gramps would be standing there.

But nothing happened.

Charlie put the wreath on the step and rushed away.

When Charlie came home, he
found Mother Pig ready to take the
little pigs sledding.

The big sled carried them quickly
down the hill. They didn't mind when
the sled tipped. They squealed with
delight as they rolled in the soft snow.

On the way home, they passed the house of Grumpy Gramps. Charlie's wreath was hanging on the door.

Charlie was happy.

Now Christmas might come to Grumpy Gramps.

A wonderful smell of baking greeted Mother and the Pig children when they got home. Father had been busy making delicious Christmas treats. He had set some aside for the children to nibble because sledding made the little pigs very hungry.

Then Father fetched a big box of decorations from the attic. The Pig family hung brightly colored balls, stars, glittering ornaments, and garlands of silvery tinsel on their Christmas tree.

They even hung yummy candy canes.

Charlie thought of Grumpy Gramps. Christmas without
a tree! How could Christmas come to Grumpy
Gramps if he didn't have a tree?

Charlie found a branch that had been cut from the tree. He stuffed it in a flower pot and decorated it.

It wasn't a whole tree, but it did look nice.

Grumpy Gramps needs some goodies, too, thought Charlie.
Mother helped him fill a box with gingerbread elves, apple tarts,
cookies covered with red and green sugar, nut bread, candies, and
all sorts of treats.

But how could Charlie get the tree and the box of goodies to Grumpy Gramps? He was too small to pull the big sled.
Charlie had an idea.

All was quiet and dark at the
house of Grumpy Gramps.
Charlie wasn't scared this time.
He pulled his little sled up the
path and left the tree and the box
of goodies on the step.

Now Charlie was very sure
Christmas would come to
Grumpy Gramps.

It was Christmas eve. Carolers came to sing to the Pig family. Mother gave them steaming cups of hot chocolate. Charlie offered them cookies.

Charlie could see the little tree in the distance. It sparkled in the window, lighting the house of Grumpy Gramps.

Sally, Toby, and Charlie hung their stockings
on the fireplace. They put out a glass of milk and
a plate of cookies for Santa.

All was ready.

Snuggled under his blanket, Charlie lay awake listening for the sounds of Christmas. He waited for the sound of Santa and his reindeer on the roof. But he never did hear anything, because he soon fell fast asleep.

Anyone passing the house of Grumpy Gramps that Christmas eve would have been very surprised. The house was no longer quiet. It was no longer dark. All night a light shone, and there was banging and clattering from within.

What could Grumpy Gramps be doing?

Then it was morning. Sally, Toby, and Charlie jumped out of bed and raced to see what Christmas had brought.

Oh, my! What a sight! There were presents for everyone heaped around the tree. Wrapping paper was ripped quickly from boxes and packages.

In the midst of the excitement, the pigs heard a loud knock. Father opened the door. There stood Santa.

"Ho! Ho! Ho!" said Santa. "I have been told that a very kind little pig named Charlie lives in this house. I have a special present for Charlie."

Santa reached in his bag and brought out a beautiful little sled. It was the perfect size for Charlie.

Then with a cheery "Ho! Ho! Ho! Have a very merry Christmas," Santa went on his way.

Charlie was puzzled as he watched Santa shuffle away. Something about the way he walked seemed familiar. Charlie couldn't think whom he looked like.

Can you?